S0-APN-934

Faith
the
FLOWER
Friend

K R I S   M A R X H A U S E N

LIVE
DIO DOWNLOAD INCLUDED

Faith the FLOWER Friend

tate publishing
CHILDREN'S DIVISION

KRIS MARXHAUSEN

Published by Tate Publishing & Enterprises, LLC
127 E. Trade Center Terrace | Mustang, Oklahoma 73064 USA
1.888.361.9473 | www.tatepublishing.com

Tate Publishing is committed to excellence in the publishing industry. The company reflects the philosophy established by the founders, based on Psalm 68:11,
"The Lord gave the word and great was the company of those who published it."

Book design copyright © 2013 by Tate Publishing, LLC. All rights reserved.
Cover and interior design by James Mensidor
Illustrations by Alexis Domin Limpiado

Published in the United States of America

ISBN: 978-1-62510-311-6
1. Juvenile Fiction / Religious / Christian / General
2. Juvenile Fiction / General
13.06.25

A child was sent from heaven above,
placed in her parents' arms to love.
Faith was the name they gave to her
a miracle, they knew for sure.

Faith was special among boys and girls, running around with bouncy curls.

She got into this and into that
and found a flower to put on her hat.
Flowers here and flowers there
painted flowers upon her chair.

As she skipped on the
backyard grass
she saw tiny flowers with
a magnifying glass.

She plucked a flower,
placed it in her hair
then walked down the
street with a tiny flare.

A smile Faith had for those she met,
a cute happy girl they
would never forget.

Faith picked many flowers,
made a special bouquet.
to share God's love when
she gave them away.
"Here is a flower grown just for you,
a smile from Jesus and
His saving love, too."

With her flowers all gone,
to home she'd return.
Those flowers gave reason
to live and learn.
Faith touched the hearts
she met that day,
choosing Jesus was the only way.

Faith was known as the Flower Friend,
to those whose broken
hearts she'd mend.

"See God's love in the beauty of a flower, know God's love in its everlasting power."

listen|imagine|view|experience

AUDIO BOOK DOWNLOAD INCLUDED WITH THIS BOOK!

In your hands you hold a complete digital entertainment package. In addition to the paper version, you receive a free download of the audio version of this book. Simply use the code listed below when visiting our website. Once downloaded to your computer, you can listen to the book through your computer's speakers, burn it to an audio CD or save the file to your portable music device (such as Apple's popular iPod) and listen on the go!

How to get your free audio book digital download:

1. Visit www.tatepublishing.com and click on the e|LIVE logo on the home page.
2. Enter the following coupon code:
   ce7b-ee39-a137-2442-7cc1-7d02-8cd8-fa46
3. Download the audio book from your e|LIVE digital locker and begin enjoying your new digital entertainment package today!